Jo was Mum's sister. She was
getting married.

Wilma was happy. She wanted to
be a bridesmaid.

Wilf was unhappy. He didn't want
to be a pageboy.

The grandparents came. They came for the wedding.

"What a journey!" they said.

Mum made Wilma's dress.
Grandmother helped.

Wilf looked at the material.
"Oh no!" he thought.

Grandmother made the cake.
Wilma put a bride and groom on it.

"It's wonderful," said Jo.

Wilma's dress was finished. Biff
and Chip came to see it.

"I like weddings," said Chip.
"I don't," said Wilf.

Jo took Wilf's measurements. She
gave them to Mum.

Wilf was unhappy. He didn't want
to be a pageboy.

Mum had been shopping.

She had a surprise for Wilf.
"What is it?" asked Wilf.

"It's a suit," said Mum.
"You're not a pageboy," said Jo.

"It was a joke," said Grandmother.

It was the day of the wedding.

Dad made a video. Biff took a
photograph.

Wilf liked his suit. He was glad he
wasn't a pageboy.

He was happy. Everyone was
happy.

There was a big party. Everyone danced.

"I like weddings," said Wilf.

"Will you get married?" asked Wilf.
"I don't know," said Wilma.